This book belongs to

_ _ _ _ _ _ _ _ _ _ _ _

_ _ _ _ _ _ _ _ _ _ _ _

_ _ _ _ _ _ _ _ _ _ _ _

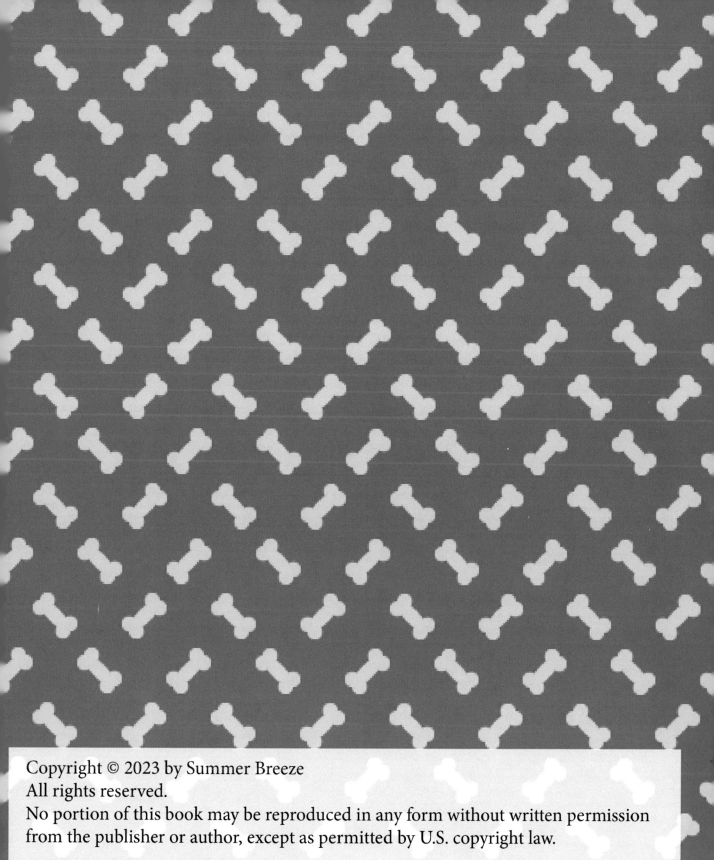

Always Bee Yourself Unless It's Halloween

Dedicated to Winter Blue, Midnight Storm, Caribou Calhoun

and Willow Wren.

Thank you for loving me unconditionally, teaching me more

than I could ever teach you, and keeping me laughing.

To my immediate and extended family that are dog lovers,

and to my dog loving friends nationally and internationally.

To my one true legacy Blaise, Westin, and Colton.

You are the daily reminder why life is worth living, and you

gave me the best title anyone can have, Mom.

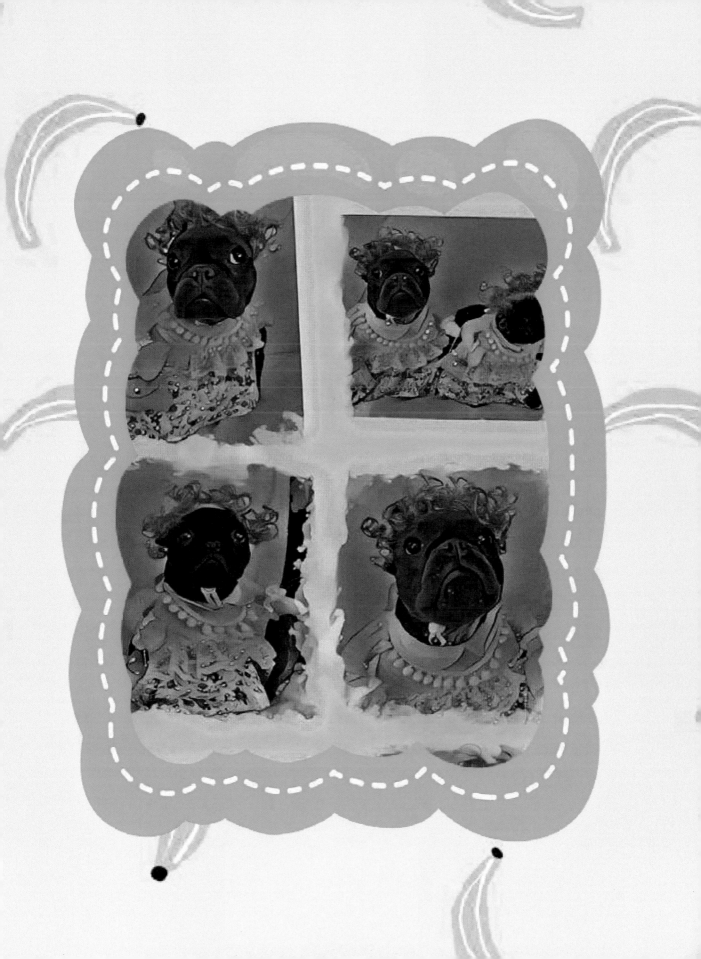

Halloween was almost upon two robust Frenchie's Midnight and Winter. The excitement was building up with candy, costumes, and haunted houses. The smell of sweet apples, and candy corn filled their house. Halloween was a big deal to their parents, and they took costumes very seriously. Winter thought maybe she was getting too old for trick or treating. Winter, you are never too old for Halloween. Betty White always said "The older you are the better you get, Unless you're a BANANA "

Midnight came up with the idea of them both going as crocodiles with spikes on their backs. Winter would have to be the mamma crocodile while Midnight would be the baby crocodile. They liked this idea, but needed to keep exploring their options. They loved the idea of saying after a while crocodile, catch you later alligator. Something their family always said to them.

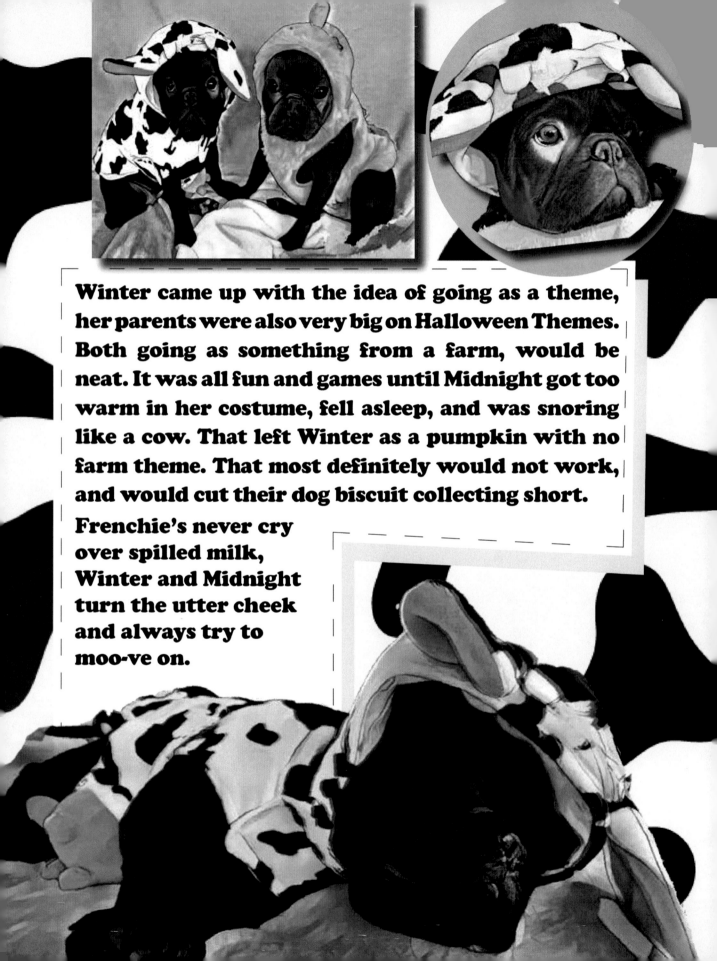

Winter came up with the idea of going as a theme, her parents were also very big on Halloween Themes. Both going as something from a farm, would be neat. It was all fun and games until Midnight got too warm in her costume, fell asleep, and was snoring like a cow. That left Winter as a pumpkin with no farm theme. That most definitely would not work, and would cut their dog biscuit collecting short.

Frenchie's never cry over spilled milk, Winter and Midnight turn the utter cheek and always try to moo-ve on.

Midnight thought she had come up with a brilliant idea. Let's go as The Nightmare Before Christmas. We are always getting into trouble, making messes, and tearing up toys. All we would have to do is put on Santa hats.

We ARE The Nightmare Before Christmas, literally. Winter said that's too easy Midnight.

Dashing through the Snow

Winter then said, hey I got an idea. Let's go as the Sanderson Sisters from the Hocus Pocus movie.

Midnight said she didn't want to do that. Everyone would think she was that black cat from the movie.

It's all just a bunch of Frenchie hocus pocus. Regardless, Winter thought she made a perfect costume of Winifred Sanderson.

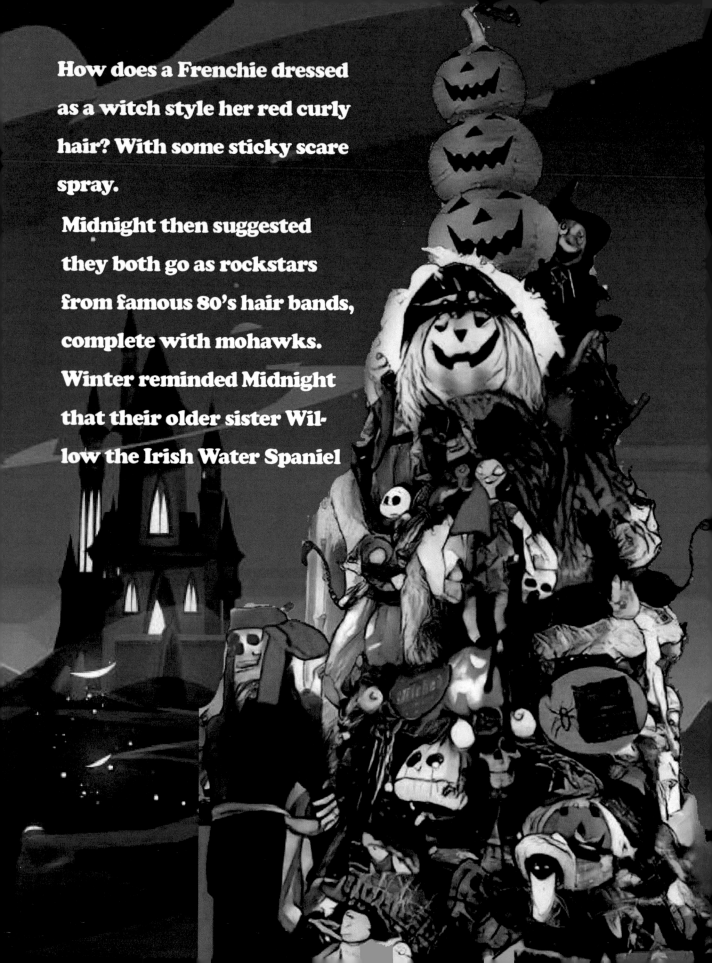

How does a Frenchie dressed
as a witch style her red curly
hair? With some sticky scare
spray.

Midnight then suggested
they both go as rockstars
from famous 80's hair bands,
complete with mohawks.
Winter reminded Midnight
that their older sister Willow the Irish Water Spaniel

went as that last year and she would be mad if they copied her.

Willow went around saying I won't be a rockstar I'll be a legend that Halloween. What type of music do Irish Water Spaniels wrapped up as old mummies prefer on Halloween night? Only wrap music, of course.

You could go as a lion Winter, said Midnight. With all the surgeries that you have been through, and all your health issues. You have the heart of a lion. Living through things that most Frenchie's have not. A lion sleeps in the heart of every brave Frenchie. If you ever feel the need to be an animal in this world, be a lion and let them hear your roar. How did the Frenchie dressed up as an angry lion stop the scary movie she didn't like? She found the remote and quickly pressed paws.

Winter suggested, how about we just stay in on Halloween night. We can watch spooky movies, eat movie theater popcorn, and sit by the roaring fire in jammies. That sounds wonderful said Midnight. We need to be careful who we pick as our babysitter, you know how those movie scenes end.

Where do fashionable Frenchie's that are dressed as spooky ghosts shop for their outfits? In little B👀-tiques, of course.

They both remembered that they had lobster costumes, and they could both go as that this year. They had already gone as lobsters the year before and they thought maybe everyone would recognize them from the previous year, so they opted out of that idea. Their Frenchie parents couldn't think of anything "butter" than their two lobsters with claws. Lobsters love to party their claws off during the holidays because 'tis the sea-son for them.

Winter told Midnight, they always say to BEE yourself, unless it's Halloween. We could go buzzing around the neighborhood as worker bees. Mom always says to BEE careful not to drop our dog biscuits Midnight said otherwise, we will be called a fumble bee, instead of a bumble bee. What did the adorable Frenchie dressed as a busy buzzing bee say to the naughty Frenchie dressed as the non-working bee? You better start to bee-hive yourself, or else.

They both thought it would be fun to go as wick-ed witches in orange party dresses. Since, after all we are the life of the party said Winter.

Winter decided that Midnight looked amazing in the color orange because she was as black as night. Winter is a blue Frenchie and she didn't think she looked particularly good in orange. Plus, how would we ever get our brooms to fly. What do you call two Frenchie Bulldog witches that live in the same house? Bestie Broom-mates!

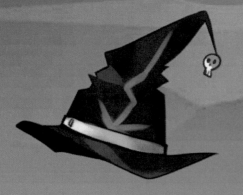

After a full day of trying on all their favorite costumes, exhausted and overwhelmed with options, they had finally decided what they were going to go as. Their final decision was to go as wicked cute Frenchie's that do whatever they want. The spoiled babies that ride in a leopard print Halloween stroller. Besides they are all clowns without any costumes. Happy Haunting!

Dedicated to all our fur babies that we adopted that are no longer with us, and have crossed over the rainbow. Also, our two Frenchie's, and our two Irish Water Spaniels. Last but certainly not least we can't forget all the French Bulldog owners, Irish Water Spaniel fans, and pet lovers who adopt and give homes to homeless pets every day!

You all know who you are.

Thank You!

Made in the USA
Las Vegas, NV
09 December 2023

82446801R10017